Fashion:
The Stories That Clothes Tell Us

Contents

1	Clothes tell stories	2
2	5000 BCE–30 CE: From peasants to pharaohs	4
3	130 BCE–1453 CE: How silk shaped the world	6
4	1300s–1600s: Europe gets a "makeover"	8
5	1526–1827: Jamas and daffodils	10
6	1600s and 1700s: Showing off sideways	12
7	1700s: Women want trousers!	14
8	1837–1901: A tale of two childhoods	16
9	1920s: Fun for flappers	18
10	1850s–1950s: Suits and kimonos	20
11	1960s: The Swinging Sixties	22
12	1990s–present: Can fashion save the planet?	24
13	What stories will our clothes tell?	26
	Glossary	28
	Index	29
	A fashion timeline	30

T0318098

Written by Alice Harman

Collins

1 Clothes tell stories

Clothes keep us warm, protect us from the sun, celebrate our **culture** and lots more.

In this book, we'll look at how clothes can tell us about the time, place and culture people live in. We'll explore how fashion can connect history's dramatic events and world-changing ideas to the everyday reality of people's lives. We'll uncover the fascinating stories of how styles and materials became fashionable, and see how different people's clothes hold clues about their role in society.

And remember, we're living through history right now!
Our clothes tell stories, just like those from the past.
As you read, try to think about what those stories
might be – and what
we can learn
from them.

2 5000 BCE–30 CE: From peasants to pharaohs

In ancient Egypt, clothes told the story of two different ways of living in the same place and time. Ancient Egypt, like many societies in the past and present, had a small number of very rich people and a large number of very poor people.

Most people in ancient Egypt worked extremely hard, growing and making food in order to survive. They typically wore simple, naturally white cloths wrapped around their body. At the other end of society was the pharaoh, the all-powerful ruler of ancient Egypt.

We're not sure whether ancient Egypt had strict rules about what different people in society could wear. However, most people could never afford dyed, patterned fabrics or precious jewellery, which is why only rich people wore them.

The pharaoh and their family lived in palaces and wore colourful clothes and precious jewellery.

pharaoh

3130 BCE-1453 CE: How silk shaped the world

As centuries passed, people around the world discovered new techniques for creating fabric and developed new clothing styles to wear it. However, the divide between rich and poor continued.

People in China began making and wearing **silk** clothes more than 2,000 years ago. Chinese silk, in beautiful colours and patterns, became famous and fashionable in many far-off countries because of its incredible softness and shine.

a 12th-century Chinese painting showing women ironing newly woven silk cloth

Traders began travelling thousands of kilometres to buy silk in China and sell it in Europe and other places. The twisting network of routes they took through the mountains of Central Asia became known as the Silk Road.

As people journeyed between countries, selling silk and other goods, they also spread new ideas, technologies, religions and even diseases. Cultures connected and mingled together, weaving their separate histories into one global future. The story that silk clothes tell is of how fashion ended up bringing many countries closer together.

4 1300s–1600s: Europe gets a "makeover"

Hundreds of years later, Renaissance Europe had a great desire for new, luxurious fashions. However, the story that Renaissance clothing tells can't be separated from other things that were happening at the time – in art, buildings, writing and science. Renaissance fashion was just one part of a whole way of seeing the world – wanting everything to be the very best.

Renaissance means "rebirth". At this time, Europe was trying to follow the example of the ancient Greeks and Romans 1000–2000 years earlier. Essentially, that meant thinking big and making things beautiful. What people wore changed, along with the new, exciting ideas they learnt about. However, as usual, only wealthy people were able to afford the latest, luxury fashions.

Notice the rich colours, materials and patterns in the clothes and surroundings of this wealthy family and their servants.

9

5 1526–1827:
Jamas and daffodils

The clothes of the Mughal Empire – which stretched across modern-day Afghanistan, Pakistan and India – tell the story of a busy, well-connected part of the world. A place where it was fashionable to mix local traditional dress, like the long-sleeved jama tunic, with **influences** from other countries.

These are European flowers, copied from prints brought to the Mughal Empire. This fabric is part of a hunting coat that a wealthy man in the Mughal Empire would have worn around 400 years ago.

Rich, powerful men often wore heavily decorated coats or jamas. This man's outfit combines traditional Mughal elements, such as the sash-like patka around his middle, the "pajama" trousers and the turban, with the European-inspired flower design of his jama and the **Persian** influence of his curled-toe shoes. Foreign elements like these suggested he had a knowledge of the world and its fashions, either through travel or education.

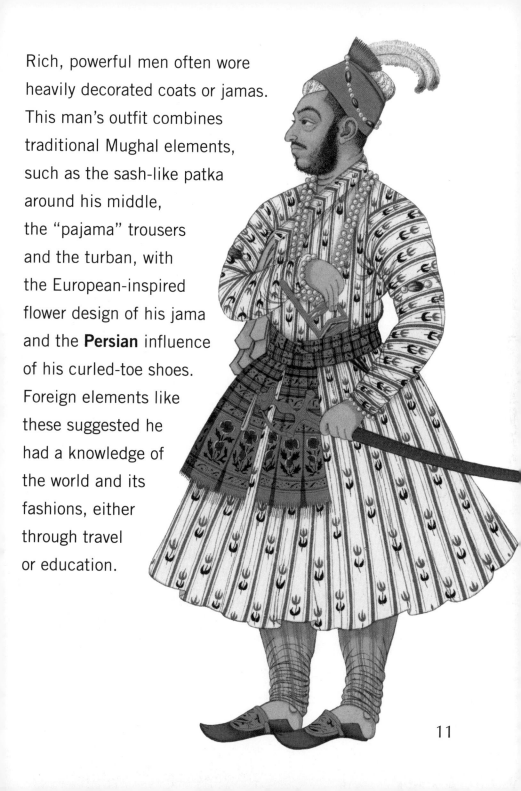

6 1600s and 1700s: Showing off sideways

Rich European women in the 17th and 18th century courts had to spend a lot of time learning how to walk and dance in a heavy, uncomfortable dress called a mantua. Even putting it on was a struggle, with the layers of stiff, hooped **petticoats** and hip pads needed to support the oversized skirt.

All this effort was really about showing off the dress's rich silk fabric. A big, beautifully decorated dress displayed how rich and fashionable you were, so the wealthiest women wore extra-wide dresses.

It took a very, very long time to stitch all this decoration by hand.

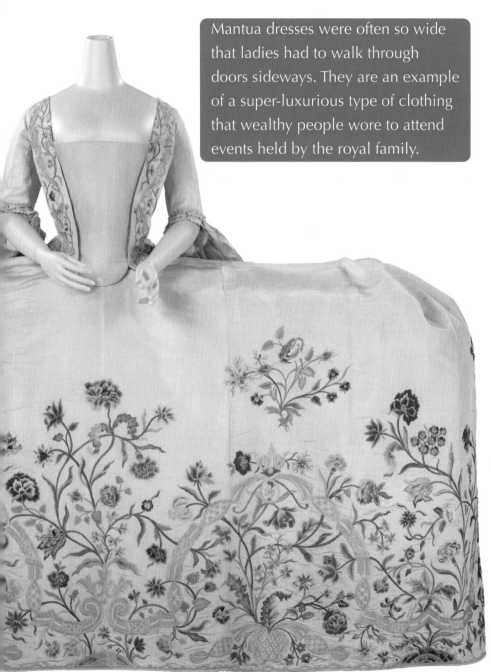

Mantua dresses were often so wide that ladies had to walk through doors sideways. They are an example of a super-luxurious type of clothing that wealthy people wore to attend events held by the royal family.

7 1700s: Women want trousers!

When more women from Europe started visiting the **Ottoman Empire** around 400 years ago, they found that the women there had more freedom and rights than they did. They also saw women wearing more comfortable clothes, like şalvar, rather than the tight **corsets** and wide, heavy skirts they were expected to wear.

A woman wearing şalvar – trousers traditionally worn by men and women in the Ottoman Empire.

The visiting women wanted this, too! So trousers became a symbol of the struggle for equality and **women's rights**. Within about 100 years, they caught on as a trend for women in Europe.

8 1837–1901:
A tale of two childhoods

Discomfort wasn't always a choice for people, however. When Queen Victoria ruled England, many children's families couldn't afford to buy them shoes. At the same time, some families got much richer and showed off their wealth by buying brand-new, fashionably frilly clothes for their children.

Poor children's clothes and shoes were plain and comfortable, constantly mended and worn by child after child until they fell apart.

Children's clothes show the two sides of the Industrial Revolution, a time when big **factories** started taking over from small businesses that were making things by hand. Some people, like this family dressed up for teatime, had new opportunities to make more money and live more comfortably.

However, most people still worked very hard but were barely paid enough to keep their family housed, fed and clothed. The factory owners got rich from the workers' hard work, and sometimes their children's work too, while the workers struggled in poverty.

9 1920s: Fun for flappers

Despite trousers being introduced into Western fashion in the 1700s, for a long time Western fashions for women had involved wearing a corset to make the waist smaller. However, in the 1910s and 1920s, the "straight-up-and-down" look became fashionable, skirts crept up from floor to knee, and fashion became fun.

No one knows exactly what the word "flapper" means, but the flapper look tells the story of an exciting moment for women in many countries around the world. The First World War was over, the nights were filled with new kinds of music and dancing, and young women were living more independent lives in their free-flowing dresses. Many people had more money to spend on fashion and fun, although there were still lots of poor people struggling to survive.

These women, with their "cloche" hats, short haircuts and straight dresses decorated with scarves, are the height of 1920s "flapper" style. At the time, it was quite shocking!

19

10 1850s–1950s: Suits and kimonos

In contrast, around 400 years ago, Japan closed itself off from the rest of the world, to stop European countries taking over. For around 200 years, no one was really allowed in or out of the country, and Japan didn't **trade** with other countries.

In the 1850s, the USA threatened to attack Japan with its boats if it didn't agree to trade. So, Japan opened up to the world, but its time in isolation meant it had a very strong, unique culture. That culture included Japanese people wearing a special patterned robe called a kimono. Japan's leaders worked hard to modernise the country. Part of this involved taking on some Western ways of doing things, while keeping Japanese traditions alive.

The mix of clothes in this 1940s photo tells the story of Japan's changing culture. The mother and older girls are wearing traditional kimonos, while the father and younger children are in Western-style clothing.

11 1960s: The Swinging Sixties

Look at this dress's fun pattern! It tells a story of how young people, in the USA and beyond, tried to change the world. They wanted to break rules from the stuffy old past in everything from politics and music, to art and fashion – and have fun doing it!

Although most 1960s clothes were still made of fabric, a fashion developed to make dresses out of paper, which seems to have changed the way people thought about fashion. Many people believe that the idea of "**fast fashion**", which is having such a terrible effect on Earth and climate change, started in this decade.

Traditionally, people had thought of clothes as expensive things, worth taking care of and wearing for a long time. But dresses made of paper, ordered from a magazine and sent in the post, made clothes cheap and fun to wear a few times, and then throw away.

an example of a paper dress from the 1960s

12 1990s–present: Can fashion save the planet?

The trend for fast fashion has continued into the 21st century. Fast fashion, in which huge amounts of clothing is made, worn and thrown away, is hurting both our planet and many people who make these clothes in unsafe, unhealthy conditions.

Sustainable fashion means producing fewer, higher-quality items of clothing that are made to last. It also means making sure that workers are safe and fairly paid, and that clothes are made in more **eco-friendly** ways. This involves using natural and recycled materials, and changing processes to reduce waste and avoid using harmful chemicals. We still have a long way to go, but we're getting on the right track.

Farmers growing **organic** cotton don't have to risk their health, or hurt nature, by using harmful chemicals.

This designer outfit is made out of wild **nettles**!

13 What stories will our clothes tell?

It's hard to think of ourselves as living through history, but some day, children will learn about how people dressed today, and what it said about the way we lived.

We are alive at a very important time for our planet, where our clothes can either be part of the problem or the solution. Turning away from fast fashion gives us a chance to be more creative and help Earth all at once.

We can **upcycle** our clothes, mix **vintage** clothing from different times in the past, buy second-hand clothes, and learn skills from online videos to decorate our outfits and keep them looking great for longer.

Rather than being told what to wear by large fashion companies, we can decide for ourselves how our clothes will tell our own unique story. What story might your clothes tell?

Glossary

corsets stiff, tight pieces of clothing to shape the waist

culture shared language and customs of a particular group of people

eco-friendly designed to be better for the environment

factories buildings where machines make products

fast fashion a way of producing and selling clothes quickly and cheaply

influences ideas that have spread to other cultures

nettles plants covered in tiny hairs that sting when you touch them

organic grown without using harmful, human-made chemicals

Ottoman Empire a huge, powerful state that controlled parts of Europe, Asia and north Africa from around 1300 to 1922

Persian what is now modern-day Iran

petticoats skirts worn under an outer skirt

silk fabric made from cocoons of soft, strong thread, spun by silkworms

sustainable fashion a way of producing and selling clothes that tries to limit damage to Earth

trade buying and selling, or exchanging, goods

upcycle decorate or redesign something to make it better or more useful

vintage clothes from the past, usually second-hand

women's rights freedoms and powers that women deserve – to enjoy the same quality of life as men, for example and to vote

Index

ancient Egypt 4–5

art 8, 10

Asia 6–7, 10–11, 20–21

children 16–17, 21, 26

China 6–7

coat 10, 11

colour 4, 5, 6, 9

dress 12–13, 18, 19, 22–23

Europe 7, 8–9, 10, 11, 12, 14–15, 20

fabric 5, 6, 10, 12, 22

fast fashion 22, 24, 26

flapper 18–19

Industrial Revolution 17

jama 10–11

Japan 20–21

jewellery 4–5

kimono 20–21

mantua 12–13

men 11, 14, 21, 25

Mughal Empire 10–11

Ottoman Empire 14–15

patka 11

pattern 5, 6, 9, 20, 22

poor 4, 6, 16, 17, 18

Renaissance 8–9

rich 4, 6, 9, 11, 12, 16, 17

şalvar 14–15

shoes 11, 16

silk 6–7, 12

Silk Road 7

skirt 12, 14, 18

sustainable fashion 24–25

trousers 11, 14–15, 18

women 6, 12, 13, 14–15, 18, 19

A fashion timeline

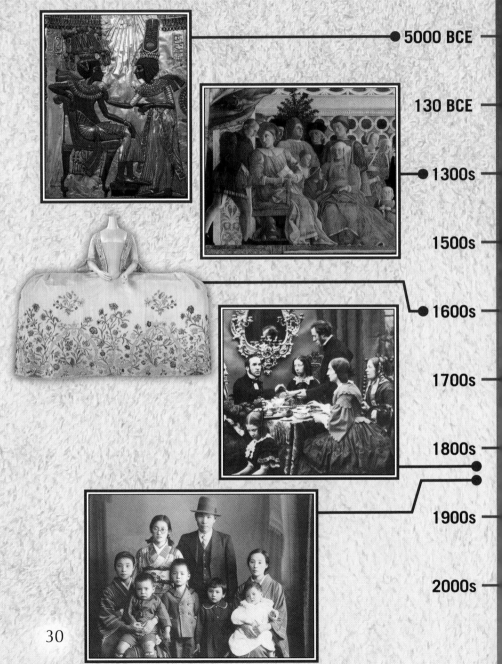

- 5000 BCE
- 130 BCE
- 1300s
- 1500s
- 1600s
- 1700s
- 1800s
- 1900s
- 2000s

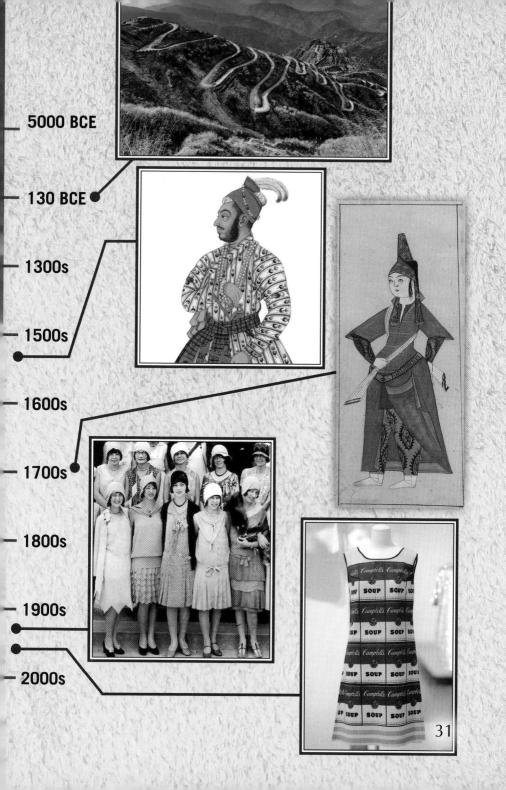

5000 BCE

130 BCE

1300s

1500s

1600s

1700s

1800s

1900s

2000s

31

 Ideas for reading

Written by Gill Matthews
Primary Literacy Consultant

Reading objectives:
- check that the text makes sense to them, discussing understanding and explaining the meaning of words in context
- ask questions to improve their understanding of a text
- retrieve and record information from non-fiction
- participate in discussion about both books that are read to them and those they can read for themselves, taking turns and listening to what others say

Spoken language objectives:
- ask relevant questions to extend their understanding and knowledge
- use relevant strategies to build their vocabulary
- articulate and justify answers, arguments and opinions

Curriculum links: Design and Technology

Interest words: problem, solution, unique

Resources: recycled materials

Build a context for reading

- Ask children to read the title and look at the picture on the front cover. Ask them to describe the different clothes each person is wearing, and establish that it's a visual timeline of changing fashion.
- Read the back-cover blurb. Ask children how they think fashion can reflect what is happening around the world. Encourage them to support their responses with reasons. Discuss how they think clothes might be able to tell a story.
- Point out that this is an information book. Explore children's knowledge and understanding of features such as contents, glossary and index. If necessary, show them where these are and demonstrate how to use them.
- Ask children what they think they will find out from the book.

Understand and apply reading strategies

- Ask children to find and read the contents page. Ask what they notice about how the book is organised. Ask them to turn to the chapter called *Clothes tell stories*.